MY LIFE IN 2055

MY CITY IN 2055

CARRIE LEWIS AND CHRISTOS SKALTSAS

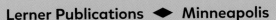

Lerner Publications ◆ Minneapolis

Lerner Publications Company
An imprint of Lerner Publishing Group, Inc.
241 First Avenue North
Minneapolis, MN 55401 USA

For reading levels and more information, look up this title at www.lernerbooks.com.

Main body text set in Mikado a Light
Typeface provided by HVD Fonts

Library of Congress Cataloging-in-Publication Data

Names: Lewis, Carrie (Children's author), author. | Skaltsas, Christos, illustrator.
Title: My city in 2055 / Carrie Lewis ; illustrated by Christos Skaltsas.
Description: Minneapolis : Lerner Publications, [2021] | Series: My life in 2055 |
   Summary: "Electric vehicles and wireless charging stations, energy from solar
   panels and wind turbines, deliveries by drone or robot—these are some of the things
   we might see in the city of the future!"—Provided by publisher.
Identifiers: LCCN 2020023447 (print) | LCCN 2020023448
   (ebook) | ISBN 9781728416304 (library binding) | ISBN 9781728423531 (paperback) |
   ISBN 9781728418551 (ebook)
Subjects: LCSH: Cities and towns—Forecasting—Juvenile literature. | City and town
   life—Forecasting—Juvenile literature. | Smart cities—Juvenile literature.
Classification: LCC HT152 .L49 2021 (print) | LCC HT152 (ebook) | DDC 307.7601/12—
   dc23

LC record available at https://lccn.loc.gov/2020023447
LC ebook record available at https://lccn.loc.gov/2020023448

Manufactured in the United States of America
1 - 48862 - 49197 - 7/29/2020

TABLE OF CONTENTS

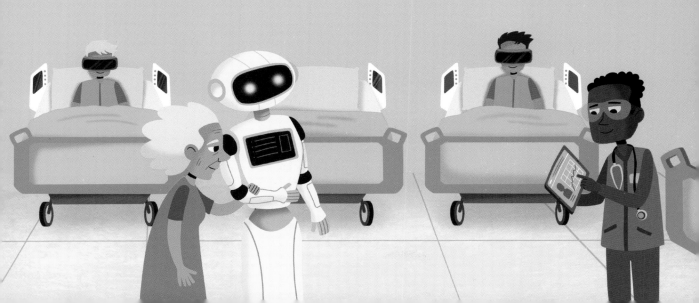

REAL OR IMAGINARY?

Let's take a look at the future of cities.

People are always coming up with ideas about how we can live better and make our environment healthier.

Cities of the future might look like the ones in this book—but then again, they might not!

While you are reading, pause and think about what you've read. What would your city of the future be like?

WELCOME TO MY CITY!

This is a typical city in 2055. When you look closely, you might see some things that are new to you.

One thing you will definitely see is that some of the biggest buildings are covered with leaves and flowers. These plants absorb carbon dioxide and give off oxygen. They keep the air fresh!

These gardens are also really good for insects and birds. There is always lots of wildlife.

LET'S FIND OUT SOME MORE ABOUT CITIES IN 2055.

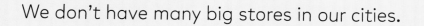

We don't have many big stores in our cities.

Our downtown has a lot of places to eat and get your hair styled, but not as many places to shop. This is because most people buy things online.

Downtown has many offices, but it also has a lot of fun places. People come downtown to enjoy themselves.

There are some parks and a library. If you need something in particular, then the librarians can help you find it online.

Entertainment downtown is free!
We have a big stage where people
can watch a play or listen to music.

7

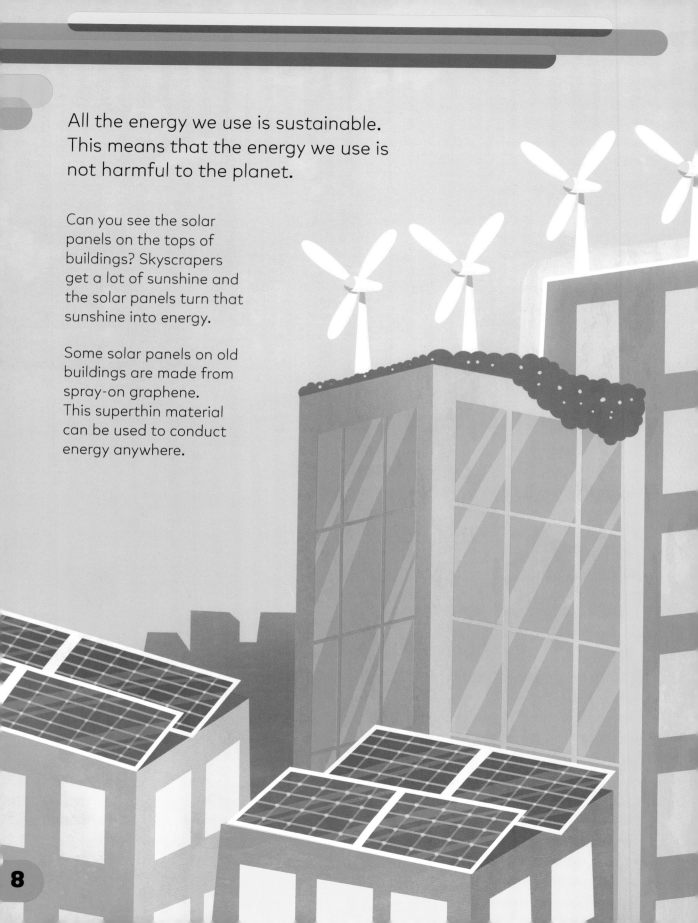

All the energy we use is sustainable. This means that the energy we use is not harmful to the planet.

Can you see the solar panels on the tops of buildings? Skyscrapers get a lot of sunshine and the solar panels turn that sunshine into energy.

Some solar panels on old buildings are made from spray-on graphene. This superthin material can be used to conduct energy anywhere.

We also have wind turbines. Houses have small turbines, but buildings have bigger turbines to create even more energy.

GETTING AROUND IS FUN!

There are still cars in 2055, but not that many.
Instead, we have other ways to get around town.

Looping around the center of town is an electric monorail.
It has no driver—it's autonomous.

There are also electric trams and buses. They travel from
the suburbs into the city center.

The roads have wireless chargers. This means our electric cars can charge while they drive.

Our streetlights are not on all night. They only turn on when someone is coming. Everywhere you go, you are always in the spotlight!

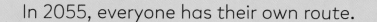

In 2055, everyone has their own route.

If you go on foot, then you can walk in the long, green parks that run all the way through town. In the spring, they are full of flowering plants.

If you ride a bike or a scooter, then there's a path for you.

Finally, there's the road. This is for the automatic delivery trucks and cars that need to move quickly around the city.

We don't have many accidents. Cars, bikes, and walkers are all much happier when they are not all sharing one noisy, busy road. People can talk as they walk and they don't need to worry about crossing the road.

13

WE CAN EAT THE WHOLE WORLD

That sounds greedy—but it's really delicious!

We like to eat food from all over the world. Some areas of town have food from India, some from China, and so on for as many different types of food as you can think of. There are wonderful smells in every neighborhood.

ITALIAN

14

We eat out a lot. Everyone likes to meet their friends and family to eat and talk.

In the past, people ate a lot of takeout, but the meals came in plastic and paper containers and made a lot of waste. Now people take their food home in reusable containers to reheat, or they sit in a cafe or restaurant to eat.

THAI

INDIAN

MEXICAN

WHAT DO WE DO FOR WORK?

Do you think that in the future all work will be done by robots? It's not! People still work.

A lot of people in 2055 grow food. We have urban farmers who work in large aquaponic farms. Aquaponic farms use the waste from fish as food for plants. The plants also clean the water to send back to the fish tanks. It's called a symbiotic system.

We also have engineers, designers, IT workers, teachers, doctors, and nurses. We have a lot of care workers to look after the elderly too.

People often work until they are over 70. This keeps people's brains and bodies active and healthy.

In 2055, we have hospitals with doctors and nurses, but we don't have neighborhood doctors.

When you are ill, you go online and fill out a questionnaire. A doctor who is working remotely will review your answers and tell you what to do next.

If it's something serious, then you go to the hospital. The hospital has scanners, x-ray machines, and equipment to diagnose your illness. Using your health data, a personal package of treatment is made for you.

Our hospitals have movie lounges, theaters, spas, and companion robots to keep people company. There's even a virtual reality (VR) lounge so that people can pretend to be somewhere else. People get better faster when their brains are active and happy.

19

People still break the law in 2055.

A lot of crime is cybercrime. The police discover it by tracking people online.

The police also catch criminals out and about. In 2055, sensors can easily track people's movements. You can even tell which room of a house someone is in. The police track criminals through buildings. They also watch their phones and cars.

Our security systems prevent home robberies. But some stores and other buildings still get robbed.

LET'S TALK TRASH! WHO EMPTIES THE BINS?

We try to make as little waste as possible because we don't want things going to the landfill.

Nearly all our waste is recycled. When we finish using something, whether it's a cereal box or a worn out pair of socks, we recycle it.

We have a fabric recycling bin and a paper recycling bin, and there are bins for glass, plastic, and kitchen waste, like potato peel. Anything that we can't clean, like old tissues or kitchen sponges, go in a separate bin.

All the waste gets taken away by an self-driving garbage truck. Then the waste is sorted, cleaned, and sent to places where it can be made into something new.

WHAT ARE PARKS LIKE?

In 2055 we know how important plants are for keeping the air clean. Green areas are also great for keeping people happy.

Our parks include a lot of trees. Ash and willow trees grow quickly and produce a lot of oxygen. We grow these everywhere so that the air stays fresh.

Parks aren't just for looking at! They are for living in too. Our parks have a lot of wild areas where we don't cut the grass or control the weeds. This means that birds and insects have safe places to live. Keeping chemicals away from plants is a good way to protect important insects, like bees, that play an essential role in our ecosystem.

WHAT'S THAT BUZZING NOISE IN THE AIR?

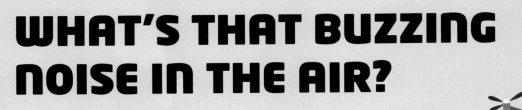

Don't worry, it isn't giant bumble bees!

The buzzing noise comes from delivery drones. These carry things to people's homes. If we need something delivered quickly, we order it online and then the drones drop it off at our houses.

Fragile orders are carried by delivery robots that travel along the ground. It took us a while to get used to seeing these around. Now these delivery robots are part of our city!

There are also police and traffic drones. These watch certain buildings or roads.

27

WE'RE NOT COMMUTERS— WE'RE A COMMUNITY!

In 2055, we work close to home.

Commuting long distances isn't good for the planet because driving causes pollution. It isn't good for people either. Commuting is stressful and makes people spend time away from their families.

Working close to home means we have more time for family, for ourselves, and for our community.

Being part of a community means being together. We garden and play together. We share our food and help each other out.

In a community, neighbors can look after one another.

TOGETHER IS A GOOD WAY TO BE.

GLOSSARY

aquaponic
Farms that use waste from fish in tanks to grow food.

cybercrime
Crime that is committed online.

ecosystem
A system of plants and animals that rely on each other.

graphene
A strong and thin material that electricity passes through.

landfill
Holes in the ground where people put waste products.

sustainable
Materials and systems that can be used and maintained without causing damage.

symbiotic
Two things that depend on each other.

turbine
A rotating device that converts wind into energy.

LEARN MORE

If you want to know more about technology of the future, here are some places to start.

Johnson, Steven. *How We Got To Now*. New York: Viking, 2018.

How Stuff Works Website
https://www.howstuffworks.com/

London Science Museum Website
https://www.sciencemuseum.org.uk/objects-and-stories/everyday-technology

National Geographic Website
https://www.nationalgeographic.co.uk/cities-of-the-future

Science Kids Website
https://www.sciencekids.co.nz/technology.html

Smithsonian Website
https://www.si.edu/Kids

INDEX